Zebra
LITTLE

First edition 2007

Copyright © 2007 Anno Domini Publishing
1 Churchgates, The Wilderness, Berkhamsted, Herts HP4 2UB
Text copyright © 2007 Catherine House
Illustrations copyright © 2007 Olwyn Whelan

Publishing Director Annette Reynolds
Editor Nicola Bull
Art Director Gerald Rogers
Pre-production Krystyna Kowalska Hewitt
Production John Laister

ISBN: 978-1-59325-094-2

Published in 2007 in the US and Canada by The Word Among Us Press
9639 Doctor Perry Road Ijamsville, Maryland 21754
www.wordamongus.org
800-775-9673

Printed and bound in Singapore

Little Zebra

by Catherine House and Olwyn Whelan

Little Zebra was born just as the first raindrops fell on the dusty plain. "Come on, Little Zebra. You need to get up!" her mother said gently.

Little Zebra was finding it difficult to stand on her thin, wobbly legs. Her mother gave the foal a little push with her nose. With a big effort, Little Zebra stood up and looked all around.

As Little Zebra stared, the other zebras turned and stared back. "Well, that is a surprise!" one of them whispered. "A little white zebra without any stripes!" grunted another. Little Zebra could not hear the whispers. She was too busy having a bath.

9

A few weeks later, Little Zebra stopped playing with the other foals.

She seemed very quiet.

"What's the matter, Little Zebra?" asked her mother.

"I'm not the same as everyone else," mumbled Little Zebra as tears filled her eyes. "I don't have any stripes. Why am I different?"

Her mother lifted her head. Someone was coming toward them.

"Little Zebra, your father is here," she said quietly. "You can ask him."

The large, strong zebra looked down at his daughter with kind, brown eyes.

"I'm not the same as everyone else," said Little Zebra. "I don't have any stripes. Why am I different?"

"Come with me!" her father replied. "I want you to meet some other zebras. They will help you find your answer."

"Here's my special friend, Old Zebra."
The zebras nodded their heads to say hello.

"Old Zebra is the only one I know who has white stripes rather than black ones."

"Why are you this color?" Little Zebra asked.

"I don't know," laughed Old Zebra. "But I do know that God made me. He gave me these special stripes, and he loves me just the way I am."

Then Little Zebra and her father went galloping across the plain until they met another family of zebras.

"We came from the far country," the zebra family explained. They showed Little Zebra their pale legs and their unusual stripes.

"Why are your stripes so different?" Little Zebra asked.
"We don't know," they answered. "But we do know that
God made us. He gave us these special stripes, and he loves us
just the way we are."

"Every Zebra is different," Little Zebra's father explained. "Our ears are different from one another. Our manes are different. And every zebra has a different set of stripes. But it doesn't matter what we look like—we are all zebras, and we need each other."

In the sky, an eagle was circling. Little Zebra's father looked up.

"Because you have a white coat, you will have to be very careful.

You must always be on the lookout for those who hunt us. I want you to be a watcher for the herd. Will you do that for me?''

19

From that day on, Little Zebra thought about her father's words.

She began to watch the long grass at the edge of the water hole, in case someone was hiding there.

She watched the antelopes to see if they were grazing peacefully or if they were worried by something.

Little Zebra began to sniff the air. Within a short time she could recognize the different animal smells that came her way.

"Little Hyena! I know you are hiding behind that rock," she laughed. "You can't hide from me. I can smell you anywhere!"

Then one day the wind brought a new smell.
Immediately Little Zebra raised her head.
The long grass was moving in a strange way.

The antelopes nearby began to run toward the forest.
Raising her head, Little Zebra cried out as loud as she could,
   "Run, everyone! Danger!"

At once the other zebras stopped feeding. The mothers and their foals began to gallop away. At that moment two lions sprang from the long grass. They were too late.

The herd of zebras was now on the move. The lions could not catch them. They chased the zebras for a while but soon gave up. Everyone was safe.

Some time later, Little Zebra was playing with her friends. "Why don't you have stripes like us?" one of them asked.

At first Little Zebra didn't know what to say. Then she saw Old Zebra down by the water hole. The family from the far country was standing nearby in the shade of a thorn tree.

Little Zebra lifted her head proudly.

"I don't know why I don't have stripes," she answered. "But I do know that God made me, and he loves me just the way I am."

MITRA MODARRESSI

YARD SALE!

DORLING KINDERSLEY PUBLISHING, INC.

To my family

Dorling Kindersley Publishing, Inc.
95 Madison Avenue
New York, New York 10016

Visit us on the World Wide Web at http://www.dk.com

Dorling Kindersley books are available at special discounts for bulk purchases for sales promotions or premiums.
Special editions, including personalized covers, excerpts of existing guides, and corporate imprints
can be created in large quantities for specific needs. For more information, contact Special Markets Dept.,
Dorling Kindersley Publishing, Inc., 95 Madison Avenue, New York, New York 10016; fax: (800) 600-9098.

Library of Congress Cataloging-in-Publication Data
Modarressi, Mitra.
Yard sale / written and illustrated by Mitra Modarressi.
p. cm.
"A DK Ink book."
Summary: When Mr. Flotsam has a yard sale in the quiet town of Spudville,
his neighbors are first upset, then delighted by their purchases.
ISBN 0-7894-2651-X
[1. Garage sales—Fiction.] I. Title. PZ7.M7137Yar 2000 [E]—dc21 99-27592 CIP AC

The illustrations were created with watercolor. The text of this book is set in 18 point Granjon.
Printed and bound in U.S.A. First Edition, 2000
2   4   6   8   10   9   7   5   3   1

Spudville was a quiet town. The houses were clean, the yards were neatly mowed, and people kept to themselves. Nothing strange ever happened in Spudville until . . .

One Saturday a hand-written notice appeared around town: YARD SALE! it read. TODAY ONLY! MR. FLOTSAM'S PLACE, 99 CROOKED HILL ROAD. No one could remember a yard sale in Spudville before. They decided to check it out.

YARD SALE!
TODAY ONLY!

MR. FLOTSAM'S
PLACE

99 CROOKED HILL ROAD

"Howdy," Mr. Flotsam said as people began to arrive.
"I cleaned out my basement and figured I ought to have a sale."
Things were a bit rickety and worn, but the prices weren't bad
and everyone left with something they really wanted.

But by the next morning things started to get a little peculiar. The Zings' new living-room rug flew out the front door, along with their son, Max.

Miss Milton's new typewriter zipped off page after page of its own writing.

When Mrs. Applebee's new telephone rang, it was her great-great-great-great-great-grandmother, just calling to say hello!

Frannie Frumkin's new music box wouldn't stop playing a hopping polka that kept her family dancing all morning.

When Mr. Twitchett planted some of the seeds he had
bought, he instantly found himself surrounded by a garden
of monstrous proportions.

And when Mr. Rotelli tried out his pasta maker, it seemed to be missing its OFF button.

The whole town was in a tizzy. By noon a crowd of people had gathered at Mr. Flotsam's to demand their money back, but he was nowhere to be found. Taped to his door was a note that read GONE TILL NEXT SATURDAY.

"He's a crook," Mr. Rotelli said to no one in particular.

"What did he sell you?" Mr. Twitchett asked.

"Come and see." And Mr. Rotelli led everyone back to his house.

By then the noodles were waist deep. "Appalling!" said Miss Milton.

"Delicious!" said Nellie Crumb, who had helped herself to some strands. Everyone tried a bite, and they all agreed that it was the best-tasting spaghetti they had ever eaten.

"You call this a problem?" Mr. Twitchett said. "You should see what *I* got stuck with." And so the group followed Mr. Twitchett down the road to his house. "Look at what's happened to my nice orderly garden," Mr. Twitchett said with a sigh.

"What a jungle," the crowd murmured.

"Not a jungle—a jungle gym!" squealed the children, and they started climbing and swinging and dangling from the large vines. Everyone complimented Mr. Twitchett on his green thumb, and he beamed with pride.

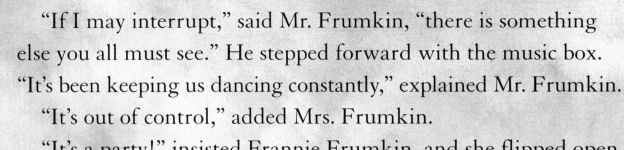

"If I may interrupt," said Mr. Frumkin, "there is something else you all must see." He stepped forward with the music box. "It's been keeping us dancing constantly," explained Mr. Frumkin.

"It's out of control," added Mrs. Frumkin.

"It's a party!" insisted Frannie Frumkin, and she flipped open the box to prove it. Suddenly everyone was jitterbugging around Mr. Twitchett's yard and out onto his patio. They formed a conga line, and Mr. Rotelli had them doubled over with laughter as he did the funky chicken. When Frannie finally shut the music box, they all agreed that it was the best party they'd been to in years.

"It's a truly remarkable music box," said Mrs. Applebee,
"but something *very* odd is going on at my house." The crowd
followed Mrs. Applebee, whose phone was still ringing off the
hook when they got there. "Don't answer it," she warned. "That
phone is haunted. The last call I got was from Amelia Earhart!"
The crowd took a step back.

"We should get rid of it," someone whispered.

"Let's answer it!" said Henry Haley, and he grabbed the
receiver.

Henry found himself talking with a singer named Elvis. It turned out they got along famously, and they even sang a rocking version of "Blue Suede Shoes" together.

After that, people were lining up to use the phone. "I can't wait to talk to my dear mother," Mr. Frumkin said.

"And I can finally get my great-great-great-aunt Sylvia's recipe for carrot cake," said Mr. Rotelli.

"One at a time," said Mrs. Applebee, who was beginning to grow more fond of her amazing new telephone.

"What a fascinating item," said Miss Milton, "but you must see what I bought."

"To Miss Milton's!" Mr. Twitchett shouted.

Inside, the typewriter was still clattering away and the stack of papers was growing. "It kept me up all night," complained Miss Milton.

"How annoying," sympathized Mrs. Frumkin.

"How interesting!" said Ned Quigley, who had begun to read some of the pages. They passed the sheets around, and they all agreed that the typewriter had real talent.

It was then that the crowd saw the Zings, hurrying down the street. Everyone went outside.

"It's our son, Max!" cried Mrs. Zing.

"He's been stolen away by our living-room rug," explained Mr. Zing.

"Oh, my!" the crowd exclaimed.

"We should form a search party," Miss Milton suggested. But then they noticed a figure up in the sky, moving closer and closer. It was Max!

"That was great!" he shouted as he glided to the ground. His parents ran over and hugged him. Soon all of the children were lining up to take Max's rug out for a spin.

After that day, things were never the same in Spudville. The Zings' rug was always in great demand. . . .

The Secrets of Spudville by Miss Milton
(and her typewriter) was on the best-seller list
for a record thirty-three months.

Mrs. Applebee, now known as Madame Olga, enjoyed a steady stream of visitors to her parlor, thanks to her new telephone.

On Friday nights everyone gathered at the Frumkins' home for an evening of dancing.

Mr. Twitchett opened his garden to the public and let the
children have full run of the place. He passed along his produce . . .

. . . to Mr. Rotelli, who used it at his Ristorante Rotelli, which got a four-star review in the *Spudville Standard*.

And as for Mr. Flotsam, the next time spring rolled around, he decided to hold another yard sale. . . .